The Fire Lights of Christmas

a Firehawks romance story

by

M. L. Buchman

Buchman Bookworks

Other works by M.L. Buchman

The Night Stalkers
The Night Is Mine
I Own the Dawn
Daniel's Christmas
Wait Until Dark
Frank's Independence Day
Peter's Christmas
Take Over at Midnight
Light Up the Night

Firehawks
Pure Heat
Wildfire at Dawn
Full Blaze

Angelo's Hearth
Where Dreams are Born
Where Dreams Reside
Maria's Christmas Table
Where Dreams Unfold
Where Dreams Are Written

Dieties Anonymous
Cookbook from Hell: Reheated
Saviors 101

Thrillers
Swap Out!

One Chef!
Two Chef!

SF/F Titles
Nara
Monk's Maze

1

"Rise and shine," **Patsy** Jurgen swept down the hall of the Cascade Hotshots barracks. This was their first wildland firefighting season, the newest hotshot team in the country. And the worn-out, board-and-batten building was their new home. She thumped the side of her fist once on each wooden door, making them rattle loudly on old hinges.

She smiled to herself. It had taken her six years to make foreman of an Interagency Hotshot Crew and this was about the nicest place she'd ever lived.

She'd heard some of the new recruits griping good-naturedly about a "hardship post." Once the fire season hit, they wouldn't be in residence here in Leavenworth, Washington all that often. And after their first month or so walking to the wildfires, they'd bless having running water, a cot, and a roof that only leaked a little.

After two weeks of recruit selection and three more of intense training, the twenty hotshots had really come together. The old hands and the new were blending well. They had yet to be tested by anything more strenuous than a prescribed burn to cut fuel levels in untended fields around the mountain town, but she knew the real thing would be happening all too soon.

Not soon enough for her.

Candace Cantrell's phone call that she was forming up the Cascade IHC had brought Patsy running. Cantrell had been a kick-ass foreman on the San Juan IHC and Patsy wanted to lead her own crew someday. She couldn't ask for a better slot than being Cantrell's foreman, her Number Two. Of course she had to share that particular slot, one super and two foremen to a crew.

Jess Monroe, the other foreman, opened his barrack door before she could thump it.

"Yeah, yeah! I'm up already, Jurgen." He didn't look it, but she knew from overlapping him on various crews over the years that he wasn't a morning person and the only thing that really woke him up fast was a fire. He wore shorts, and nothing else. He was hotshot fit, muscle rippled along his legs and chest.

"Day one, Monroe." Candace had just informed her team last night that she'd let the Forest Service know the Cascade IHC was ready for call out. A real testament to her skill as a superintendent that they'd trained up so fast, because Patsy agreed. They were ready.

"Day one," he looked down at his watch. "Still early yet. Wanna come in and celebrate?" He held the door a little wider. As foreman, he had a room to himself instead of a two-bunk, just as she did.

"I think you're still dreaming, Jess." The man would flirt with a burning tree.

He never pushed; teasing women was just some kind of a game to him. Most flirted back and they all seemed to have fun with it. A skill she'd never had nor wanted. She reached out and pulled his door shut—with him on one side and her on the other.

It wasn't *that* early. She'd woken everyone just early enough to ease into it and eat before the day's planned exercise.

Candace and Luke Rawlings, one of the newest recruits, had gotten a small apartment also close by the fire station. The heat between them was amazing to watch; it was just so…right. Candace had always been deadly serious about hotshotting; fire chief's daughter, no big surprise. But with Luke she glowed like, well, like she was happy.

Patsy hadn't seen that one coming at all. Candace was so dedicated to wildfire that she had become a role model for Patsy. Her suddenly finding love was like a crack in Patsy's worldview—one she still didn't know what to do with.

Patsy had woken before sunrise, an old habit, and gone outside to watch the day break before waking the others. The sun had lit the towering peaks of the Cascade Mountains which climbed up to the west of Leavenworth eventually topping out at Stevens Pass. The line of sunlight had moved down the conifer and gray rock-covered slopes like the slice of a knife, the line was so clean. To the east, the mountains fell away into hills headed for the rolling sagebrush and orchard steppes of Eastern Washington.

On the silent air, broken only by a blue jay's call, the scent of pine washed through the river valley. Dry pine. It was only June, but already she knew it was going to be a hot summer and a busy fire season. They'd been smart to sponsor a hotshot crew here.

Now that everyone was awake, but not moving yet, she was suddenly at loose ends. So she walked the couple blocks into the sleeping town; hadn't had a moment to breathe during training to give it the once over. All of her prior postings had been pretty far out into the nothing. "Town" usually meant a church, a grocery store that was also a gas station, and a pizza joint that was more importantly the sole bar. But here, the Cascade hotshots had been formed by Chelan County and posted in a resort town surrounded by towering timber.

Leavenworth was…bizarre. A failing timber town in the 1950s, it had resurrected itself as a Bavarian Alps village in the 1960s and been a tourist mecca ever since. The kitsch was so complete that it was almost believable. She wondered if even Bavaria looked this German.

Coming east from the fire station, just a block off Route 2—the second biggest east-west highway across the Washington Cascades—she walked right into the heart of "old town." A gazebo on the village green. Red brick cobblestone paving with ornate black cast-iron streetlights. White buildings with that zig-zag dark wood accenting. Generous balconies that dripped with massive red geraniums.

Every building that didn't boast a beer garden was lush with souvenirs. There was a lederhosen store for crying out loud and, she'd seen in the few breaks they'd had from training, that it did a serious business.

Tourist kids tromped around town with an ice cream cone and wearing attire right out of *The Sound of Music.*

The only thing open at this hour was the Bavarian Bakery. She was missing breakfast, eggs and bacon no doubt, most of them taking white toast. Why was it that hotshots had no imagination about food? They certainly had to eat enough calories to survive a fire season, but they always went for the fastest and the easiest.

As she walked by the bakery's window, someone slid a tray of delicacies into the display. When the baker saw her hesitation, he flashed her a big smile and waved her to come inside.

The tray looked fantastic.

2

Sam Parker waved at her again.

The woman watched him for a long moment, then shrugged and turned for the door.

"First customer and not a tourist. For that you get an extra special treat," he greeted her before the bell even stopped jangling. Not a local either. He'd only bought the bakery a month ago, but there was something in the way she moved that was different.

A tourist rubber-necked and wandered, and if they were up at this hour of the morning then they'd be wearing their runner's togs. Seattle folks who didn't know how to slow down for even one second.

A local would be moving with purpose and direction. This woman had been out strolling at sunrise for the sake of strolling.

"Smells good," she'd stopped one step inside and sampled the air. Most went straight to the big display cases brimming with confectionary. Or headed straight for the register to order their triple-shot skim macchiato, which wasn't a macchiato at all.

Instead she remained where she was long enough to let him really get an eyeful. Her honey-blond hair was short-cropped, and offset her dark eyes. Her face was thin and well-tanned though it was still more late spring than summer.

She wore a yellow shirt and cargo pants with big thigh pockets and serious boots. He could see the power of her despite the loose clothing just in the way she stood.

"I give up." Nobody back in Providence, Rhode Island had ever come into his shop looking like this. He couldn't make sense of her outfit.

She slanted a look over at him, but didn't say a word.

"What are you?"

She raised an eyebrow.

Okay, maybe not the best greeting, so he waved a hand at her attire rather than risking more words. He ran a bakery, words were almost as important as sugar to making a success of it, but he didn't know which words to use with this woman.

She inspected herself carefully and then looked back at him, again raising that single eyebrow. Without the least hint of a smile, she answered, "*Homo sapiens,* female of the species."

At Sam's burst of laughter, she barely blinked.

3

While he laughed, Patsy turned back to inspect the display cases. Most bakeries smelled of sugar, sugar, coffee, and more sugar. But just as a wildfire had hints of cedar, redwood, pine, maple, and a hundred other clues, the air of the Bavarian Bakery was deeply nuanced.

The sugar was there. And the chocolate. But she could smell the butter in the croissants, the apricot in the Danish before she spotted it, the smoothness of rich Bavarian cream, the sharp cinnamon in the baked apple strudel. Hotshots were always lean, there was simply no way to consume more calories than you burned during a season; often there simply wasn't time to do so. But this was a place a woman just might have to be careful. It all looked as incredible as it smelled.

The baker hadn't gone back behind the counter, but instead had remained out front with her. She knew what he'd meant of course, had received the question so many times over the years that the straight answer had long since worn out any interest for her.

A hotshot? What's that?

I fight wildland fires.

Forest fires? Like a smokejumper?

Yes, but without the parachute.

I thought that was a guy thing, jumping out of planes.

As if she hadn't just said…

Sure, hotshots were predominately male. The upper body strength required meant a woman had to want it twice as badly as any man to make the grade—had to bust her ass to overcome genetic predisposition.

Not as unusual as it once was.

It was common now for a hotshot crew to have at least a couple women. The even more strenuous smokejumper roles were starting to see women on the crews as well.

She'd grown so tired of all the stupid follow-on questions, that she'd stopped answering the first one. But usually the men knew she was avoiding a straight answer, grew offended, and left her alone.

This one had laughed, a good laugh. It made her glance back over when she didn't intend to. He didn't look like a German baker: round-faced, blond-haired, and all of the other stereotypes in her brain. He was as lean as she was, an inch or so taller, and his big hands and powerful arms showed a hundred small burn scars and a few older ones that weren't so small. Working with fire. She knew how that looked; had her own fair share of them.

"*Homo sapiens,* male of the species," he answered her apprising look.

She could feel a smile tugging up one corner of her mouth. The man had a sense of humor, and he worked with heat. Even if it was in another form, it was intriguing in its own way.

4

Sam pushed himself up the trail. He'd left the bakery at noon, after a typical nine-hour day, baker's hours. And he enjoyed unwinding on the hiking routes that abounded so close to Leavenworth that he could walk to the trailheads. In Rhode Island, the biggest hill had been eight hundred feet and been a half-hour drive away, when Providence traffic felt like cooperating. Now he lived at twelve hundred feet and couldn't turn around without seeing a half dozen eight thousand footers.

During his one month here, he'd learned that hiking the Cascades was a different challenge than back East, and not just the elevation. A wrong turn there could lead you back to the highway miles away from your car; do the same thing here and you could walk a hundred miles without ever seeing another human, or a road. Wilderness that even jets took a while to cross over. Lost on foot?

Very bad news.

Today, he headed off across the flats to the south of town. He'd spotted a plume of smoke up on the hills and used it as an excuse to hike in a new direction. A boxy truck was parked at the base of the trail. Light green with shining golden script, *Cascade Hotshots.*

It was an odd vehicle. The back was a short box with four windows down the sides, like a bus that had its back end sawed off. But instead of being on a bus frame, it was on a very heavy duty truck form, like a cement delivery truck—robust enough to tackle serious loads. Or, he noted that it was parked well across the fields from the nearest street, to negotiate rough terrain. The ride did not look comfortable.

He continued up the trail, the breeze and sun at his back as he climbed. The trail became steep and tough, but he'd learned, and now wore solid boots rather than light walking shoes.

Sam rapidly ascended above the meadow line into the wooded hills, and thought of the woman from this morning.

"Funny how someone can stick in your mind," he told a nodding bush, pulling out his guide long enough to identify it as a huckleberry. He'd have to come back and pick some once they were ripe. He often talked to himself, or at least to the surrounding wildlife as he hiked.

And though he didn't want to be noticing a woman, any woman, she really had stuck in his head. Christi had left him with a gaping wound after a brutal divorce that had sent him all the way to this remote mountain village seeking a bolt hole.

Last thing he wanted was to be noticing a woman.

But when he'd watched her eyes flutter shut in appreciation as she bit into his apricot almond bear claw…

Then snap open when her pager buzzed loudly. A quick glance at the small device on her waist and she completely changed.

The slow-moving, slow-smiling woman evaporated as if she'd never been. Now she was pure business. She folded the bear claw in half and stuffed one end of it into her mouth but didn't bite it off. With her hands free, she dug out her wallet, tossed him a ten dollar bill, and bolted out the door without either her hot chocolate or her change. Maybe she was an ambulance EMT or something. Whatever, she'd simply evaporated.

"Maybe that's what was so intriguing," a chipmunk looked at him doubtfully from its hesitant perch atop a boulder. "My woman of mystery."

The chipmunk laughed and scooted.

So much for that idea.

He rounded a bluff and stumbled to a halt.

He'd been hiking steadily upward through thick conifer forest. His East coast brain would call it a pine forest, but his assistant at the bakery informed him that it was mostly fir trees out here. He'd rounded a boulder in the trail, and the world changed. Before him lay a scene from Dante's *Inferno* so jarring that the transition made little sense.

The low grasses and tall trees were gone, replaced by black char. The trees up ahead were tangled with fire. Flames circled and swirled up the tall trunks, heaving ash into the dark cloud of smoke overhead. A gust sent a spray of embers aloft that danced like fireflies against the black smoke and shining flame before reluctantly winking out. It was beautiful and horrible at the same time.

He looked back over his shoulder. Sun-dappled forest.

He turned ahead once more…

There were figures moving about the base of the flames, people in yellow hard-hats and coats.

The souls of the damned!

Another shower of sparks swirled aloft.

It was Hell!

5

Patsy worked down the line, checking in with her half of the crew—she and Jess each had nine crewmembers. For their first fire, they were doing well; not that it was a big one. It made for a perfect introduction.

The fire had climbed into a dead-end ravine. Candace had sent scouts both to left and right in case it tried to jump over to the neighboring ravines, but it wasn't big enough to make the leap—again, just good training. They'd think to go themselves next time after checking in with her on the radio. The fire already was dying against the walls and the only ones who didn't know it were the rooks.

The rookies saw the old hands remain calm around them—she'd alternated them down the line so that the rooks couldn't feed off each others' fear—and they had stayed calm in turn. Now it was just a matter of letting it burn out the available fuel in this narrow slot.

She broke out three rooks and a three-year veteran and led them back down to the base of the fire.

"Get a one-and-a-half inch hose into that stream over there. Start working this line. We don't want to leave a single hotspot. When this is done burning out in a couple hours, we want to have the mop-up mostly finished or we'll miss pizza back in town."

That got them moving. Nothing like the promise of real food and a place to brag about your first fire to motivate a hotshot.

A lone figure with wholly insufficient hiking gear stood at the base of the "black," as the charred area of a wildland forest fire was called, looking like he'd been electrocuted standing up. She considered climbing down to him, but decided to make him hike his pretty, clean gear up through the base of the black and save her the walk. It would stain up his boots and socks pretty good. Then maybe she'd rid herself of yet another gawker to worry about during future blazes.

She waved him up the hill to her.

He hesitated, unsure of himself until she signaled again.

As he approached, she recognized the face from somewhere. Oh, his eyes going wide as she stuffed his delicate pastry into her mouth like a some squirrel stuffing its face full of acorns.

She sighed. Graceful had never been one of her strengths.

6

Sam was only a few paces from the fire-fighter before he realized it was a woman. The charcoal smeared shirt might have once been yellow. Close-fitting sunglasses hid her eyes. Her hardhat was blue…and smeared black. The rest of the crew's were yellow.

"Why is your helmet a different color?"

The way she tipped her head when she looked at him seemed familiar, and then an eyebrow arched between her sunglasses and helmet.

"Female of the species…" came out half statement and half gasp. It was his woman from the bakery this morning. Firefighter. Wilderness firefighter.

He also recognized the half smile that tugged at her left cheek as she acknowledged him.

"Helmet is blue because I'm a foreman."

"*Foreman?* Wouldn't that be the male of the species?"

"Assistant superintendent if you prefer. The superintendent is the one over there under a hot pink helm. Also a female of the species, though she's taken." He had little more than the impression of someone moving quickly *toward* the inferno until he lost sight of her in the smoke.

Then he glanced once more at her. *She's taken* implied that the woman he was talking to wasn't, and had made a point of it. He was about to ask, but he saw the look of chagrin at her own statement, so he went for a subject change.

"Shouldn't there be helicopters and smokejumpers here?"

She glanced over her shoulder and shrugged, "It's just a baby. I wouldn't want it getting an over-inflated sense of importance. We probably wouldn't even be on it except it's a good training opportunity for a new crew."

If this was a baby, he was completely out of his league. His knees felt loose, so he sat down on a handy rise in the ground. It felt warm through his pants. Even..Hot! He jumped to his feet and brushed hastily at his butt; his hand came away black.

That smile was pulling up the side of her mouth once more.

"Okay, don't play with fire. Got the idea." The ground looked burned and black here just like anywhere else in the vicinity. He reached down to touch the ground by his boots. It felt cool by comparison.

She didn't look so amused anymore.

The woman eased him back a step and then moved forward and kicked the spot where he'd sat. A small flame burped up and was gone.

Sam swallowed against a dry throat.

She was signaling her people to come over, "Okay. See this spot?"

Her crew nodded and studied it.

She waved them back a step and used the flat hoe-like blade on the back of her fire axe to drag a gouge in it. Flames leapt upward taller than she was.

"That's what you're looking for during mop-up. Doesn't look like much, but they can be a real pain when they reignite, especially if they're behind you. Now, give me some water from the hose."

One of the people had a hose the size of their wrist that trailed back toward the stream.

As she dug into the mound, flames leapt, water shot in, steam erupted.

Sam backed off slowly, finally turned back downslope and headed away. But he kept looking back at the woman casually mopping up a fire, as fearsome as a witch on Hecate's Heath stirring her caldron.

A world of fire and steam he'd never imagined.

7

Patsy hadn't meant to ignore the man, hadn't meant to be rude, but he'd been gone before she finished the training opportunity. And fire always took precedence. They'd done well and were, indeed, back down off the mountain in time for pizza and a beer.

Candace had led them to Maxine's Pizza, a hole in the wall that had no hint of Bavarian from the outside. The insides only confirmed this was a strictly locals' joint. No waitresses in cute Bavarian skirts, no pomp and oom-pah-pah from the jukebox;

the Stones were rocking it over the speakers. She went up to the faded "Order Here" sign, and saw that the options were slices or a whole pie and a pint or a pitcher. No burgers, no soups or salads, just pizza that smelled incredible. Worked for her.

Twenty hotshots, first day on the fireline, she ordered eight large pizzas but only three pitchers—they were big here. Maxine returned her change with a smile.

"One beer each, maximum," she told the team. "You never know what tomorrow has for us." She took a diet Coke and a slice of pepperoni to wait for the pizzas to come up.

Patsy was looking for the logistics needed to pull a bunch of tables together in the crowded dining room when she spotted him. She threaded her way through the noisy area, dodged aside before one of Jess' crew took her out with the back end of a pool cue, and made it to the small table close by the stairs to the upper dining area no worse for the wear.

"May I?" He was reading something in German. Might have been a cookbook.

He blinked up at her in surprise, "Female of the species."

"Patsy Jurgen."

He said something in German that her grandmother might have understood, but was meaningless to her.

"I speak English, bad English, and worse Spanish." It wasn't that her Spanish wasn't fluent enough, it was that while she'd started her education in that language during high school, she'd finished it on the fire line. Vulgar would be putting it politely.

"Oh, sorry. Sam Parker."

"Nope!" she told him as she sat and took a bite out of her pepperoni slice, which really was as good as it smelled.

"What do you mean, *nope?*"

"You read and speak German, and you bake the best apricot almond bear claw I've ever tasted. Does that sound like a Sam Parker to you?"

"Can't say that it does," he sipped a beer. "However, Patricia Jürgen," he said it with a thick German accent, "sounds like a wildland firefighter."

"Thanks, I think. By the way, only Grandma ever called me Patricia." Conversations with attractive men often stumped her, but this one with Sam Parker…

"So, that was really a 'baby' fire?" he waved in exactly the right compass direction indicating a good sense of where he was both indoors and out. He had strong arms, looked very fit; give her a month and she could make him a damn fine firefighter.

"Good for training. This crew was only formed up five weeks ago and the season is just starting up here. Arizona is the one being hammered right now. New Mexico and Colorado will be next. Nevada and Utah don't really have enough to burn. But that's only general patterns. We could light up tomorrow. Normally we would have let the locals deal with something the size of this morning's fire, maybe send a couple of guys to assist."

He looked right and left. Looked down at his beer for a moment.

Patsy had seen this reaction before. Despite Candace's falling for a guy on her crew, that had never been her style. The problem was that someone who wasn't a firefighter never knew what to do with a woman who was.

"So you fight wildfires?"

Why did they always state the obvious before the brush-off. She nodded. Here it came.

Patsy got her feet under her so she could stand and go back to her crew. There, at least, she fit in.

Then Sam grinned at her, "Did I mention that I'm a baker? That's pretty dangerous work you know. Leave out the baking soda and you can be in a world of hurt."

In general Patsy didn't laugh much, but Sam made it easy to join in.

8

Sam wasn't quite sure how it had happened.

"Sleep deprivation, gotta be," he told the cold strudel dough he'd put in the fridge yesterday, and now pulled out onto the marble slab.

"Up way past my bedtime," he mentioned to the ovens as he lit them off so that they'd be ready for today's bake as soon as he was.

"Damn but that was a hell of a kiss," he told no one and nothing in particular.

Sam usually hit the sack at seven or eight at night and was up and in the kitchen

by three at the latest. It was four now and
he was behind.

Last night at eight o'clock he'd been
watching Patsy risk her life as she went
to snag several pieces of pizza from the
ravenous group at the hotshots' table.
He noted that she picked them up easily
though they were still oven hot, usually a
trick that only a baker could do. That she
returned from her raid unmaimed by the
hoard made her all the more impressive.

They'd spent most of the evening
bumping knees at his small table and
discovering quite how different two people's
pasts could be. Even her mom had been in
the fire business; the fire house clerk who
had married the captain. Both her brothers
rode city engines—he noted the slight
scoff in her voice—in Seattle and Boise.

He'd never been to Montana, or was it
Idaho. Idaho he decided during his second
beer around ten at night. He was the only
son of a Boston lawyer and a socialite
mother who had married into a prominent
Rhode Island family, and then gone to court
to get out of it much to his father's dismay.

They spent most of the evening laughing together. By eleven p.m. and his third beer, it was harder to stop laughing that to start. He noticed she nursed only one glass through the night, but in the laughter department she'd kept right up.

Maxine's Pizza was closer to the fire hall than his small apartment above the bakery. So, he'd walked her through the chill night air, cold enough in June to see his breath despite the lack of streetlights. They were few and far between off the main tourist strips. Whether the city fathers were being cheap or maybe they were trying to encourage tourists to stay in their part of town so that the locals could have some peace and quiet; he wasn't sure which yet.

He suspected the latter.

The nearest light had been a block away when they reached her door.

He'd considered saying some cliché about enjoying the evening.

Then he'd considered a different cliché about she was welcome in his bakery any time.

Then he'd kissed her and she'd met him halfway.

It wasn't even a first date, and he'd known her name for only three hours. But he had wanted to discover the taste of her. And though he could still scent the day's fire in her fresh-washed hair, he'd tasted the merriness of her kiss. It was as neatly hidden beneath her serious exterior as the hotspot had been beneath the char this afternoon.

It hadn't started as a friendly little kiss and it certainly hadn't ended like one. They had shared a mutual hum of pleasure before it was done.

"Good night, female of the species."

"Sleep tight, not Sam Parker."

He hadn't noticed the cold at all last night on the five-block walk home from the hotshot's barracks front door—which might have been closer to ten by the time he and his third beer were done with it at midnight. He'd been feeling very mellow and a little lost, in several ways.

For one thing, his ex-wife had left him pretty well convinced that no woman would ever want him. He'd convinced himself that he'd never again risk being with a woman. Yet he'd been here less than two months and just kissed one.

Last night. Just over that way. He glanced in the direction of the hotshot barracks and saw his walk-in refrigerator.

The three a.m. alarm had been a shocker, but he soon lost himself in the dough and a date filling, the flavor and texture, trying not to think about how much he'd like to kiss her again.

9

Patsy was unsure if she was disappointed that the fire season was off to such a slow start, or pleased that it allowed her to pursue her new morning ritual.

That second morning, returning to the bakery, had caused her to hesitate. She didn't hesitate around men, but Sam Parker's kiss the night before had been as sweet as his confections and as powerful as his flavors. It was the power of him that had surprised her, baker's arms and hands meant something, as much strength as a firefighter.

Like a good hotshot, she'd forged ahead through the door and Sam had put her at ease with his immediate smile.

Their initial greeting had been interrupted by an early jogger wanting their coffee fix.

His invitation to come to the back door the next morning had her climbing out of her bunk while the night still ruled the valley and the stars burned above.

A morning kiss, a tall hot chocolate, and the first baked good out of the oven all served on a flour-dusted counter, while she perched on a high kitchen stool was an excellent way to start the day. He was smart, funny, and enjoyed hiking. She loved his childhood memories as he prepped and baked. Day after day she'd leave him at sunrise to roust the team.

During the evenings, rather than joining the other hotshots, they would wander around town together, as if they couldn't get enough of each other. Trying out different restaurants from waffles to schnitzel. Sometimes they'd go for hikes through the lower hills in the softness of the late light once the sun had plunged beyond the tall peaks to the west. Other times they poked through the souvenir shops, marveling at the things that tourists seemed so eager to own.

There was even a year-round Christmas store right on the main square that was unbelievable. Towering trees, so thick with ornaments and lights for sale that the fake needles were barely visible except as a green backdrop. Vast Christmas villages of tiny ceramic buildings and figurines, even a miniscule skating pond with skaters. It soon became their favorite shop, as there were always new layers to discover. They would meet there before heading off to find a new place to eat. A town of two thousand people and two million tourists boasted an incredible variety of food.

Last night they had visited the animal ornaments display corner of the store and later shared a surprisingly authentic Mexican fajita. Their goodnight kiss had been the third and best element of the evening, parting at sunset as she'd adapted to his hours.

This morning Patsy had woken very early and was at the back door waiting for

him when he wandered down the stairs
from the apartment above the bakery.

He looked warm and sleepy and rumpled
—irresistibly delicious. So she didn't resist.

Sam awoke quickly enough at her
welcoming kiss in the kitchen. There was
a need that had been building in her over
these last weeks, gathering heat and starting
to burn.

"I want to take you upstairs," he
whispered against her neck.

"I want you to take me right here."

And he did. She wasn't sure what had
inspired her to slip some protection in her
pocket that morning, but she was glad she
had. With her back against the warming
ovens, his heat filling her until it felt as
if she was burning as brightly as a flame-
wreathed tree. His powerful hands were not
gentle, but neither were hers. After they'd
initially sated their bodies in a fast, bright
flare, he moved his mouth over her. As he
did, he tasted and tested like she was a fine
treat until she climbed once more over the
delicious peak and long slow waves of heat
rolled over her.

He was late to start his baking that morning, but neither of them was complaining.

10

It was their first real call up of the season and it was a hot one. Patsy's pager went off just as she was leaving the bakery feeling particularly loose and pleased with herself —and with Sam Parker.

A quick jog to the fire station and she'd found the whole crew loading up into The Box. Patsy made sure that all the gear was stowed properly from yesterday's trail-clearing work and climbed aboard with her team.

Three hours of jostling around in the back of the heavy truck later, they arrived at the base of Mt. Rainer National Park and looked up. The glacier-topped dome of the mountain was a shining beacon of light as the mid-morning sun glittered off the snow.

The fire wasn't on the mountain, but rather on the neighboring Silver King Peak. The fire had at least six heads, probably from multiple lightning strikes, that had already joined into a burn of a thousand acres. They couldn't just let it burn, because if it climbed up and over the mountain, it would take out the Crystal Mountain Ski Resort, the largest one in the state.

The primary approaches were already engulfed in the fire.

Patsy had been gearing up for the long hike in, seething with frustration at how long it would take them to get to the fire going over rough country on foot. There were no roads for The Box, not even bad ones.

Candace took one look at the situation and pulled out her radio.

"Incident Commander. This is Cascade Hotshots requesting helitack."

Of course. That's why she was the boss. Candace rocked.

Minutes later a pair of big, black-and-flame painted Firehawk helicopters from Mount Hood Aviation descended through the smoky sky and landed in the same clearing as The Box.

A man jumped down and moved past the rotors quickly, pausing just a moment to snap their photo. He looked like a goof with the two cameras—a handsome goof—but he walked like a hotshot. MHA was a top outfit, maybe he was both.

"Hi, name's Cal. Ten of you with Jeannie and me, ten with Emily," he waved at the other helicopter. "Rugged terrain up there, so you're going in by rope."

"Harness up," she shouted to the team. As soon as she had hers on, she checked her team, pleased with how little she found to correct.

Now, they were soaring aloft, packed in the back of the Firehawks like firewood, and Candace asked her, "Who is he?"

"I—" Patsy closed her mouth, unsure what to say.

"Oh, yeah. I recognize that look," Candace shouted over the helicopter's roar.

Patsy studied her boss' face, but couldn't read what was there.

"Same thing happened with Luke. There I was, going along ever so happily, and then snap!" she made a twig breaking motion. "The whole world changed."

Patsy didn't know about the whole world, but certainly a portion of it had.

She surveyed the fire as they climbed skyward alongside the steep ridges, looked at how it was moving along the hills.

Patsy pointed and Candace nodded, their first point of attack was obvious from this height—a few hundred meters from the north flank of the fire; keep it from going any wider here. Candace leaned forward between the seats to tell the pilot.

The other thing that Patsy could see was that she wasn't going to be back in time for dinner, perhaps not for days.

She pulled out her cell phone, probably no reception once they hit the ground out here in the National Park, and certainly no time. She caught two bars off a tower somewhere and dialed Sam's number.

Patsy had never had anyone to call before, when going to a fire. She'd simply go, for a day, a week, a month; it didn't matter. Once a week she tried to let Mom and Dad know she was alive, but they understood if she didn't check in during a busy fire season. They'd taught her to be safe around fire by the time she entered kindergarten. And how to fight it while still in middle school.

She got Sam's answering machine.

"Hey, this is Patsy. I'm off on a fire. Will let you know when I'm back." She didn't know what else to say. Nothing appropriate except how much she'd enjoyed having sex in his kitchen this morning. And meeting him in the evenings. And eating his delicious creations. "Uh, thanks," was the best, lame-ass thing she came up with.

Patsy hung up the phone and tucked it away as the helicopter circled down on their chosen position.

She'd be the first one down, so she clipped her rappelling harness onto the line tied off to the loop outside the cargo door.

Candace was back beside her and double-checked Patsy's gear.

"He's a baker," Patsy told her. Which explained absolutely nothing about him.

The helicopter was sliding to a halt just above the treetops.

Patsy tossed the coiled line out the cargo bay door and watched as it snaked down and disappeared through a narrow gap in the trees.

Candace's bland look told her that wasn't nearly enough explanation.

"He's really good with his hands."

At that Candace smiled and nodded enthusiastically, "Don't you just love men with good hands?"

Patsy leaned forward out of the cargo bay, then she slid down beneath the battering wind of the rotor, the fire's radiant heat powerful on her face even at this distance.

Heat. A man who worked with heat and generated it as well with those nice hands of his.

Love? She wasn't there yet, but for the first time in her life she could imagine getting there. Much the same way she could imagine beating this fire, though they hadn't even begun.

She hit the ground and disengaged from the line, but her feet were still floating somewhere up in the sky.

11

Six days.

Sam was amazed at how many emotions had churned up within him in six days.

First, disappointment that Patsy was gone and he didn't have an immediate opportunity to test if what had been between them that morning was real…or even repeatable.

This near stranger, naked and unabashed in his kitchen, had been a revelation. His first time with her had been better than any time with Christie—and throughout their marriage they'd both always remarked on how good they were together physically. Until she was also good, and unrepentant, with her married boss.

Patsy had been incredible, responding in ways he'd never imagined. And where Christie had been delicate, cultivating it into a fine, fragile art form, Patsy was powerful. She definitely gave back as good as she got, and she was impossibly, fantastically real. He'd also had no idea how amazing the body of a "female of the species" could form up until he'd had a chance to appreciate Patsy Jurgen's immense degree of fitness.

Besides, she wasn't a stranger. In their evenings together, he'd found it easy to spill out tales of his past. At first he avoided his marriage, divorce, and abandoning his job. But that too eventually came out in the comfortable world they'd created between them.

"I always wanted to own my own bakery instead of cooking in someone else's. That was about the only good thing I got out of the whole mess."

It was only after he'd said the words that he thought of how they might have sounded to this woman he was now seeing. They certainly wouldn't have met if not for his moving across the whole country to get away from Christie.

But Patsy hadn't taken some unintended offense. Instead, she'd remarked that if his business sense was as good as his food sense, he was set for life. It was good, but he'd signed up for an on-line business course that night to make sure of it.

She was more reticent than he was, but once she started a tale, she told it without any attempt to evade or be embarrassed by it. She told the good with the bad as if the past was of no consequence at all.

He worried less about the past the more time they spent together.

What he hadn't expected was to, once more, start looking forward to the future. That was a skill Christie had taken in the divorce that he was only now rediscovering.

He went through disappointment that he didn't hear from Patsy. Then anger. Surely the woman could find the damned time to text the man she'd just had sex with. Maybe that's all she'd wanted, one good screw, and was now done with him. He knew that was wrong about her, but it didn't stop it from swirling through his mind like folding a meringue time and again until it was totally flat and useless—an immensely frustrating twenty-four hours.

When he still didn't hear from her, he shifted over to fear that she'd been injured or killed and no one would know to tell him.

After two nights in a row of lost sleep, he went down to the Leavenworth fire station for lack of any better idea.

Captain Carl Cantrell was in his office.

Patsy had talked a lot, for her, about Candace Cantrell—the fire chief's daughter and head of the Cascade Hotshots. Practically worshipped the ground the woman walked on.

"Patsy?" Cantrell had offered him an easy smile. "She's still off on the Silver King Fire. Just heard from my girl last night on the radio. She thinks they'll have it contained in another day, two max. Once they can hand it off to a Type 2 mop-up crew, they'll be back, unless there's another blow-up."

On the radio. Not somewhere she could call, which could explain why Patsy hadn't called. No phone service.

Type 2? Not a clue.

At least he knew what "mop-up" looked like, columns of fire erupting from ground that pretended to be black and dead.

Blow-up he definitely didn't like the sound of.

"You the one put that smile on her face?"

Sam was tempted to avoid answering, but could feel the smile of relief on his own, knowing she was fine, just out doing her job.

"I hope that's because of me."

Cantrell just kept grinning, "Keep it up, son. That smile looks good on her. She takes it all far too seriously."

"Well, she fights fires for a living," he felt himself getting deeply protective of her.

The man held up his hands in a placating motion. "Do some of that myself."

Right, this is the Fire Chief, you dolt.

"She's a good one and I've seen enough to know. Maybe as good as my Candace, though if you say in front of my daughter I'll deny it. Just needs someone to lighten her up a bit."

Deeply comforted by the news and the Captain's words, Sam headed back into town to wait. He wanted to get her something. Something to tell her that he thought she was incredible.

As he passed the Christmas shop, he knew just what to get.

12

Back in town Patsy crawled out of The
Box and into the shower. Eight days on the
first fire of the season. She'd slept…hmm,
she was sure she'd slept at some point.
They'd *coyoted* for much of the fire, lying
down in their gear right where they finished
a shift—usually twenty-four to thirty-six
hours long—and slept until the fire made
an aggressive move and you were on your
feet again—usually way too soon.

She plunged into her first shower in all
that time and let the stink wash down the
drain with the char. Clothes in the wash.

She came to, standing upright and staring down at her bunk. Yes, she should just do a faceplant and hope nothing burned in the next twenty-four hours. But she didn't want to.

Instead, she was halfway to town before she knew what she wanted. Her brain was definitely moving slower than her body.

Eight days.

All Sam Parker had gotten from her in eight days was silence. Would he still want to see her? She thought so. She hoped so.

It was amazing how much he'd been in her head through all that time.

Instead of just living the moment of the fire, she wanted to tell him about it. The little victories, the staggering defeats, and the return to battle until it was won. There was no option, winning is what hotshots did, engaging the fire until it was down and done.

She didn't think that Sam would need a bribe in order to want her back. But she wanted to take him something to let him know she'd been thinking of him.

13

Sam had decided to hang out late in the bakery that day even though his assistants had it covered. Late morning he'd gotten a call from the Fire Chief.

"They're home. Doesn't look like they've slept much, probably shower and sack time, but I thought you'd want to know."

He left the back door open as he worked in the kitchen.

It was after lunch when a shadow cut the light pouring into the kitchen, even as he made some notes to try next time on the banana muffins.

He turned to see her, for he had no doubt it would be Patsy. Something inside him just knew.

She stood there, framed in the sunlit doorway. Instead of her fire gear, she wore shorts and sneakers that revealed those powerful legs that had been clamped so tight around his waist that one morning.

Her t-shirt was bright red with a jagged yellow line like mountain peaks, but also like fire. Block letters spelled out, "Silver King Fire" and the year. It hugged her curves in ways that just begged for him to explore them.

Her golden hair caught the sunlight like a halo of fire.

"I got you something," she held up a small bag that he recognized.

Sam reached under the counter and pulled out a similar bag, "I know it's only June, but it just seemed right."

He actually felt awkward as they exchanged bags; it was a surprisingly intimate moment. They began to open them together on the steel prep table.

He pulled out a string of lights and couldn't help smiling. It was a totally ridiculous string of tiny baked goods: cakes, éclairs, and cookies.

Sam waited while she finished unwrapping her own set of "Fiery Twinkle Lights." He snagged the plug and put it into the outlet under the lip of the counter, then he plugged in his string to hers.

Together they all flashed on and hers began to flicker like fire.

"They look good together," her voice was soft, on the verge of that rare laugh he'd so come to enjoy.

"They do," he agreed. Then he looked up at her.

"You look incredible."

"So do you," she took a step closer and nodded toward the steel prep table, the reflection doubling the lights. "It looks like between us we have a good start on a Christmas tree."

"A very good beginning," Sam moved in a step, could feel the warmth of Patsy Junger's heat spreading through him as that lopsided smile of hers broke free.

"I bet that between us, we could make an incredible tree by December." She slid into his arms and wrapped her own arms around his back. She rested her head against his shoulder.

"I'm sure you're right."

And she was.

There had never been a gift so perfect as this woman in his arms.

About the Author

M. L. Buchman has over 30 novels in print. His military romantic suspense books have been named Barnes & Noble and NPR "Top 5 of the year" and Booklist "Top 10 of the Year." In addition to romance, he also writes thrillers, fantasy, and science fiction.

In among his career as a corporate project manager he has: rebuilt and single-handed a fifty-foot sailboat, both flown and jumped out of airplanes, designed and built two houses, and bicycled solo around the world. He is now making his living as a full-time writer on the Oregon Coast with his beloved wife. He is constantly amazed at what you can do with a degree in Geophysics. You may keep up with his writing by subscribing to his newsletter at *www.mlbuchman.com.*

Full Blaze
a Firehawks romance

Cal Jackson stared up at the wall of flame eating its way toward him through the forest. He was always tempting fate one step too far. Now he was way past the second step, as well as the third. He was standing in the foreign land of totally screwed. In his seven years of fighting wildfires and five more photographing them, he'd never been this far over the line. Not even close.

He'd ridden the edge a lot since he was a testosterone-laden teen. It had earned him his fair share of cold slaps from ticked-off women, but maybe more than his share of warm and friendly nights. It had also led to numerous interesting opportunities to travel for both work and play, so he'd learned to take that risk without really thinking about it.

He tried not to take that second step very often; it was his warning that he was pushing the limits. But dancing along the edge of that step was what had won him so many of his awards. Though the Pulitzer for photography and "best of" for World Press Photo still remained out of reach, he'd bagged a lot of awards including the cover on *National Geographic*. And *Time*, twice.

Out here, way past the second step, the Grindstone Canyon Fire was in full-throated roar. The sound throbbed against his body with bass notes that actually shook his inner organs. He'd stood close beside the tracks when two-hundred-car freight trains had flown past at full speed. This was louder. Nor did it conveniently pass by and Doppler into the distance; this train of fire had him clear in its sights.

The air was growing so hot that it hurt to breathe. His acute sense of smell for smoke, burning pitch, and carbon had long since been overwhelmed by the saturation of them in the air. He'd embedded tight with a crew of hotshot firefighters who were fast losing ground against the wildfire despite their best efforts. It happened that way. Fighting fire was a delicate back-and-forth dance between flame and attacker, almost like a hip-hop advance and retreat, attack and counterattack by both sides of the…hoedown.

Hoedown? Where had he come up with that? Third foster father. Yuck!

In one way the comparison was appropriate, as it was with the rakes, Pulaskis, and even hoes that a hotshot crew used to battle the flames. Not hoedown, but rather… His brain trying to work out what hip-hop dancers called that battle of dance, power, and sensuality had to be about the damn stupidest thought to have as his last on earth.

The Grindstone in southern California was probably the last big fire of the year in the United States. The Pacific Northwest was already getting rain, and Colorado had snow, though that hadn't slowed down the Fern Lake Fire back in 2012. He'd won two awards and gotten national headlines on that one for his piece on fighting wildfires when the supply tanks and rivers froze and the helicopters couldn't get at the water to fight the flames.

The Southeast had just been soaked by a really serious trio of hurricanes. So this year California was last in the hot seat, and the fires above Santa Barbara were doing their best to take back the hills for Mother Nature. It had started in the same area of Rattlesnake Canyon Park as the lethal Rattlesnake Fire of 1953 that killed fifteen firefighters. Though this time it was started by lightning rather than a psycho arsonist.

You'd think he'd have grabbed a clue from the historical setting, though he'd been no better with history than most of the subjects in school, except fighting and photography. With maturity, he'd added "fire" as an adjective to both of them. He now knew fire history as well as any hotshot walking the hills, except for this time when it should have warned him. There hadn't been a bad burn here in more than sixty years, so it was due.

The hotshot crew he'd been with had been in the heat for a week, driving ahead and then retreating—dancing that careful strategic dance against the fire. Less than two minutes ago the crew had taken off down a narrow track leading across a cliff face and onto a rolling slope that led down into the distant valley. Their escape route was clean. He'd hesitated an extra fifteen seconds to get a shot of a massive fig tree, over eighty feet tall, being ripped up by fire-generated winds and tossed aside like a matchstick. Fifteen lousy seconds.

The problem was that the fire had cast the flaming tree down right across his escape route. The tree not only lay across the path, but was catching all of the surrounding material on fire as well. The crew looked at him helplessly across the gap.

The notch canyon that separated them was too far for a rope cast, and the vertical walls that plunged down to either side of his position required a level of mountain-eering skill that included hammers and pitons, neither of which he was carrying. He carefully eyed a ledge about ten feet below, but could think of no way to get down to it. Far too narrow a landing to risk a jump. Yet.

He could see the crew boss on the radio, but with the fire's roar, Cal couldn't hear him even though his own radio handset was in its pouch right against his shoulder and the volume was turned up to full.

The smoke blotted out the boss just as he was about to make a hand sign of some sort. A glance upward into the smoke canopy told him that no helicopters would be able to save his sorry behind. The mushroom cloud of smoke—looking like a nuclear blast it was so intense—rose ten thousand feet above the California land-scape would block any line of approach.

The ravine to the south was clogged with fire, and the one to the north was now fully lit by the thrown tree, its branches ablaze like a thousand-armed candelabra. The two ravines met to the west. The only way out was east—and there raged the beast.

The narrow ledge of his final demise was covered in a few dogwood and valley oak trees, tall grasses, and dense manzanita brush. When the fire rolled over this site, it would burn hot. Hot in the same way it had burned over the nineteen-man crew at Yarnell, the air so superheated it had burned right through their foil emergency shelters. It had done that despite the circular clearing they'd cut around themselves. And he didn't even carry a chain saw to try to make a clearing. All he had were his cameras.

He backed to the edge of the precipice and then turned once more to look at the flame. He wasn't even conscious of his actions as he lifted his new Canon Mark III camera, found the frame, shot the photo. Zoomed back. Found the next, shot it. The beast was close. He'd only once been so close to the heart of the firestorm. During his days as a member of a hotshot crew, they'd have been long gone before the heart of the fire rolled this close. The camera was actually heating in his hands, prickly hot to hold.

Too close! That was it. He dropped the camera into his bag and pulled out his old workhorse 6D body with the 28 mm wide-angle lens. No way he'd risk a lens change with all of the dust and ash in the air.

There! He could see the image coming together that would make a cover photo. Another prize-winner was almost here. Just a few more seconds… If he could just…

A metal shape zipped by the lens, fast. He didn't see what it was, but some instinct had him pressing the shutter. He flicked back to the image.

On his viewfinder a winged drone a half-dozen feet in length, painted black with gold-and-orange flames, had flown between him and the fire. It had a bold "MHA" emblazoned on its side.

Some comfort that was. All it meant was that someone from Mount Hood Aviation was going to have the award-winning photo of the journalist who burned alive while clutching his camera like a damned idiot. All because he'd had to take that third step and now couldn't wrench back from it.

Cal was going to make a lousy Cinderella, no pretty gown rising from the ashes for him. But he was sure going to end up as a cinder. Another thirty seconds and he'd have to take his chances inside the foil shelter, though he'd sworn he'd never do that again.

Maybe his life was supposed to pass before his eyes right about now, but he hoped not. He'd beaten the first sixteen years of his life down with every ounce of a fire-fighter's willpower until they didn't exist. The time since had been mostly good, but with the way his luck was running today, he'd get to see those early days before he'd named himself Calvin Jackson.

Some idiot part of him started to raise the camera again, but then he stopped. His cameras were going to cook right along with him, even if he threw himself over them like a Marine covering a grenade to save his buddies. For once he just looked at the wall of flame. Its heart so hot it glowed gold as the fire swarmed up tree trunks six stories tall with a single breath, sheathing each tree in a cloak of flame just six inches and fifteen hundred degrees thick. The roar deepened as if gathering its breath. So loud that—

The sharp blast of a voice over a loud-speaker not ten feet behind him so startled Cal that he almost stumbled off the ledge. Completely masked by the roar of the fire and with hundred-foot flames less than thirty yards away, a helicopter had come to hover behind him. It wore the same paint job as the drone.

A glance up showed the rotor blades shimmering in a lethal arc just a few feet above him and no break in the smoke-cloud cover above. The hotshot crew was still invisible across the ravine. But far down below, right off the narrow spit of cliff he was perched upon, he could see the terrain. The pilot had flown up through a hole underneath the smoke and ash cloud.

"Get aboard, you bloody git!" the speaker screamed at him. He wouldn't have heard it if it weren't less than ten feet away and aimed right at him.

The chopper hung just out of reach, hovering with its open side door toward him. Over his shoulder he could see that the spinning rotor disk was within a foot or so of a stout oak tree. They couldn't fly any closer to him. The chopper didn't even have skids to grab on to like they always did in the movies, just wheels.

The cargo bay door was an open four-by-four-foot square of salvation, hanging a half-dozen feet away over a hundred-yard drop. He stuffed both cameras into the padded bag, snapped it shut, and chucked the bag through the door toward the rear so it wouldn't go out the other side, which was also open. Then, squatting to make the leap while the chopper bounced in the roiling air currents, he jumped into space.

He landed mostly inside the door. Far enough to drag himself the rest of the way.

He spotted a rope line, made sure it was secured to something, then snapped the D ring on the front of his safety harness onto it so that he was now secure.

"Good to go," he shouted to the pilot. There was no way he could be heard. The freight train was screaming toward them, barely ten yards from the rotor tips.

The pilot, flying alone, risked a quick glance back, but was skilled enough for the chopper to remain rock stable despite the turbulent environment.

Cal only had long enough to get the impression of a narrow face and mirrored shades wrapped in a large, earmuff pilot's headset. Seeing he was aboard, the pilot rolled the chopper hard left and dove down through the dwindling smoke hole. He caught the camera bag as it skidded across the deck plating.

A glance up at the cliff showed a tongue of flame now reaching out to grab where the chopper had hovered only moments before.

Now that he was safe, the adrenaline rush kicked out hard. He'd fought fires from California to Alaska, and he'd photographed them in Brazil, Russia, and a dozen other places. He'd never before had his hands shake so badly that he couldn't even open the bag to make sure the cameras were okay. All he could do was clench it to his chest and let the shakes run through him.

***

"Yeah, Ground Command. This is Hawk Oh-two, I got him. You can release your crew to the next site."

Jeannie Clark clicked off her mike and the one-word acknowledgment came right back. She was bummed. She'd finally found a flaw with her beautiful new Firehawk. Well, almost new. The machine had done a couple tours in Iraq first, but it had been totally renovated, repainted, and reconfigured with a big belly tank for dumping retardant on wildfires. It was new to her. Her boss and MHA's lead pilot, Emily Beale, had only just certified her in this type last month. And the chopper was also new to Mount Hood Aviation's "Hoodies," one of the country's premier firefighters-for-hire contractors. It was only the second load-rated Type I helicopter in their inventory.

Until recently, she'd only been certified in the midsize Type II Twin Huey 212 and the tiny Type III MD500, both much-lower-capacity crafts. The Firehawk was built on the Sikorsky Black Hawk frame and could lift a massive thousand gallons of retardant or water, about four and a half tons. That could make a serious dent in a blaze except when Mama Nature was really kicking up her heels with Papa Fire. That was what her Australian friend Dale always called them, as if they were part of his Aboriginal Dreamtime creation mysticism. She'd looked up the expression and it wasn't, but she'd kept using it even after coming to America. People always looked at her cross-eyed when she used it, so she now kept it to herself.

The thing was, with her MD500, she could have scooted right onto that cliff edge instead of hovering out in space. Had to give the guy some points—at three hundred feet up a cliff, he'd jumped right out with no hesitation. That said something about guts, or desperation. She'd half expected him to freeze and die there. Even three more seconds and she'd have had to bug out and leave him there to burn.

Available at fine retailers everywhere

More information at:
www.mlbuchman.com